How to Save an Owl

The Wildlife Rescue Series

How to Save an Owl

Kate Messner

BLOOMSBURY
CHILDREN'S BOOKS
NEW YORK LONDON OXFORD NEW DELHI SYDNEY

BLOOMSBURY CHILDREN'S BOOKS
Bloomsbury Publishing Inc., part of Bloomsbury Publishing Plc
1359 Broadway, New York, NY 10018
50 Bedford Square, London, WC1B 3DP, UK
Bloomsbury Publishing Ireland Limited, 29 Earlsfort Terrace, Dublin 2, D02 AY28, Ireland

First published in the United States of America in October 2025
by Bloomsbury Children's Books

Bloomsbury books may be purchased for business or promotional use. For information on
bulk purchases please contact Macmillan Corporate and Premium Sales Department at
specialmarkets@macmillan.com

Library of Congress Cataloging-in-Publication Data
available upon request
ISBN 978-1-5476-1646-6 (paperback) • ISBN 978-1-5476-1647-3 (e-book)

Book design by John Candell
Typeset by Westchester Publishing Services
Printed in the United States at Lakeside Book Company
4 6 8 10 9 7 5 3

To find out more about our authors and books visit www.bloomsbury.com and sign up
for our newsletters.
For product safety–related questions contact productsafety@bloomsbury.com.

For Toby, a very good dog,
and for Samantha,
Andy, and Nora

How to Save an Owl

CHAPTER 1
The Storm

The little owl was hungry.

Chirirrrrrrup!

He called from the cavity in the craggy pine tree. It was lined with twigs and old feathers, with an oval-shaped hole for an opening. Sometimes his mother perched there, her feathers blending in with the bark. His brother, who had hatched a few days before him, was learning how to flutter up there, too.

The little owl couldn't do that yet, no matter how hard he tried. He barely got off the twigs, so all he could see was a circle of sky. As night fell, the sky circle turned from sunset pink to murky blue.

Outside, delicious insects hummed and chirped in the dusk. The owls' father was out hunting. Soon he would return with food.

What would it be tonight? A crunchy palmetto bug? A wiggly lizard? Or maybe a soft, juicy mouse!

Whatever it was, the little owl would

have to be fast. His brother always pushed him out of the way when it was time to eat.

Chirirrrrrrup!

A few seconds later, their father appeared in the opening with a little brown mouse in his talons. He dropped it in the nest cavity and flew off.

The little owl's mother tore off a piece and held it out to him. But just as he hopped over to her . . .

Snap!

His brother shoved in front of him and gobbled it up. Quickly, while his brother was swallowing, the little owl pushed his way in and grabbed a smaller piece.

Back and forth they went.

Push! Gobble!

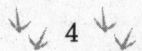

4

Shove! Grab!

Finally, when there was nothing left but tail, the little owl snuggled alongside his brother and dozed off.

A bright flash woke him up. The sky boomed and fat raindrops began to fall.

That happened sometimes on warm evenings. But this time, the wind was stronger. It howled and whipped through the trees.

The old pine tree swayed more with every gust. The little owl's heart beat fast. His feathers trembled. What was happening?

BOOM!

The wind gusted stronger and suddenly—*CRACK!*

The little owl felt himself falling. He landed with a plop on prickly wet grass as the rain fell around him. It pelted his face and matted his feathers.

Where was his pine tree? Where was his cozy nest cavity?

The little owl couldn't see anything through the pounding rain.

Where was his mother? Where was his pushy brother?

Chirirrrrrrup?

They were nowhere to be found.

CHAPTER 2
Birthday Blues

The smell of chocolate chip pancakes drifted upstairs. That was Ezra's favorite birthday breakfast. He loved how the chocolate chips got all gooey on the griddle.

Normally, Ezra was the first one awake

on his birthday, but today he dawdled. This wasn't a normal birthday. Ezra was turning eleven. Mom, Dad, and Ivy were all waiting at the kitchen table when he came downstairs.

Happy birthday to you . . .
Happy birthday to you . . .
Happy birthday, dear Ezra . . .
Happy birthday to youuuuuuuu!

Ezra yawned and looked at the clock. It wasn't even seven yet. But he forced a smile when Ivy pushed a present at him.

"Open mine first!"

"Okay." Ezra shook it, even though he

could already tell it was a book. The truth is, nothing about this birthday felt exciting. Especially the part about turning eleven. But he ripped off the paper and found a new sketchbook. "Oh, cool. Thanks!"

Ivy smiled. "I thought you could use it to draw plans for your projects."

"For sure." Ezra loved building stuff. He and Mom were planning to make a shelf for his baseball trophies. But Ezra was having trouble getting excited about that today, too.

"You look tired, kiddo." Dad set a plate of pancakes in front of him. "Did the storm wake you up last night?"

"Yeah, it was pretty loud." Ezra hadn't felt hungry, but the smell of griddled chocolate chips changed that. He dug in.

"Do you want to open your other presents now or after lunch?" Mom asked.

Ezra looked over at the wrapped gifts on the counter. His heart sank when he saw the long, skinny one. He already knew what it was.

A baseball bat. For his new league. And that was the problem with being eleven.

Last spring, Ezra had been on a team in the ten-and-under league with all his friends. But this spring, he was too old. Now he had to move up and play with the middle school kids. Ezra had watched them practicing in the park last year. They all looked way older, and they were *really* good. The first practice was tomorrow, and Ezra didn't feel ready at all.

"I'll open them later if that's okay." Ezra finished his pancakes and started to rinse his plate, but Mom took it.

"I'll get the dishes," she said. "You should go outside before it starts raining again."

"Want to play catch?" asked Ivy.

"Sure." Ezra grabbed his glove and ball, and they headed to the backyard.

The grass was still wet from last night's rain. Ezra kept slipping when he ran to catch the ball.

"Sorry!" Ivy called as she threw one over Ezra's head. It bounced into the trees

behind the house, where the grass was taller.

"Can you find it?" Ivy called.

Ezra spotted a flash of white in the grass up ahead. "Yup!"

But when he got closer, he realized he hadn't found the baseball at all. Instead, a tiny, white fluff ball of an owl stared up from the grass.

Chirrrrup!

CHAPTER 3
Predator Patrol

Ivy came looking for Ezra when he didn't return with the baseball.

"Oh!" She squatted down for a closer look at the little owl. It squinted at her. "So tiny! Do you think it fell out of its nest?"

"Probably." Ezra looked around. Sure enough, not far away was a fallen pine snag. "This old dead tree must have fallen in last night's storm. And look." He pointed to a round hole about halfway up.

Ivy crouched down and peeked inside. "There are twigs and feathers in there. I bet it was their nest." She stood up. "Where are the parents?"

Ezra searched the nearby branches, but there was no sign of them. Then a sound came from deeper in the trees.

Chirrup!

Ivy rushed over. "Here's another one!" A second fluffy owlet was peering up from the weeds.

"What did they say about baby owls in our volunteer training?" Ivy asked. "Do we put them back in the nest in case their parents return?"

"Maybe if the tree were standing. But since it fell, predators could get into that nest cavity. We should check with Mom," Ezra said. "Let's take another look to see if we can find the parents. They probably left the nest when the tree fell, but I bet they're still around." He and Ivy wandered through the trees, scanning the branches for owls.

"Come on, owls," Ivy whispered.

"They wouldn't just fly off and leave their kids, right?" Ezra said. "They must be here somewhere." A bird called over-head, and he paused to listen, but it was only the caw of a blue jay. Then quiet again.

And then, a jingling cat bell.

"Oh, no!" said Ivy as the neighbor's black cat, Tabitha, came trotting across the yard. She wore a bell so she couldn't sneak up on birds. But these little owls hadn't fledged yet. They wouldn't be able to fly away.

Ezra frowned. "Speaking of preda-tors . . ."

Ivy hurried over and scooped Tabitha up in her arms. She turned to Ezra. "We definitely can't leave the owlets here. I'll

take Tabitha home and ask the Wards to keep her inside. Do you still have the box from your new baseball cleats?"

Ezra nodded. "Good idea. And I'll see if Mom or Dad can take us to the wildlife hospital. Doc and the other staff members there will know what to do."

Ezra and Ivy's family had been to the local wildlife hospital lots of times. They were Critter Couriers, which was sort of like driving an ambulance for injured wildlife. When the wildlife hospital got a call about an injured bird or rabbit or squirrel, they'd call one of their Critter Couriers to pick it up and bring it to the hospital for care.

Once Ezra's family had rescued a

juvenile osprey that flew into someone's house and hurt its beak. Once they'd rescued a baby otter found injured on a popular biking trail. And once they'd rescued a hawk that got its leg caught in a rat trap.

This time the call for help was coming from their own backyard.

Chirrup!

Ezra ran to the house, found the shoebox, and explained the situation to Mom and Dad.

"They're probably Eastern screech owls," Mom said. "I've heard their calls out back. Wait here for a minute."

Mom hurried upstairs and came back with a small towel. "Put that in the bottom of the box to make it nice and cozy," she said. "Then lift the owlets inside, very gently, and put the lid on. They'll be less afraid in the dark."

Mom handed Ezra a pair of leather work gloves. "Use these when you pick them up. Even tiny owls have sharp talons." Then she grabbed her keys from the counter. "I'll get the car and you can meet me out front."

Ezra arranged the towel in the bottom of the shoebox and hurried back to find Ivy. She'd taken Tabitha home and was standing guard halfway between the two owlets.

"I'm on predator patrol," Ivy said. "No cats or raccoons allowed."

"Well done." Ezra lifted the lid off the

shoebox. Then he put on the gloves, picked up the first owlet, and set it gently inside. The second owlet was more active, fluttering its little wings as if it wanted to fly away.

"Easy does it," Ezra whispered as he put it in the box. It hopped right over to its sibling. Carefully, Ezra put the lid on the box and picked it up.

Mom was waiting in the driveway. "I called ahead to let Doc know we're coming," she said. "She went in early this morning because some other owlets and osprey chicks fell out of their nests during the storm last night, too."

"What will happen to them all?" Ivy asked as they turned onto the main road.

"Hopefully, most will go back to their original nests where their parents can find them." Mom glanced in the rearview mirror. "These owlets will need a new home, though. We'll see what Doc recommends."

"But their parents will still find them, right?" Ivy said.

Ezra sighed. When you took an animal to the wildlife hospital, there was no promise it would be okay. Doc and the other wildlife staff did everything they could. Lots of animals survived so they could be released back into the wild. But not all of them. Ezra already knew how Mom would answer Ivy's question.

"I sure hope so," she said. "But we'll have to wait and see."

CHAPTER 4
The Last Nesting Box

When they arrived at the wildlife hospital, Ezra's favorite volunteer Miss Alex was working the front desk. She had a phone in one hand and was filling out paperwork with the other. Two big pet carriers draped with towels sat on the floor.

Miss Alex held up a finger to let them know she'd be a minute. "And you found them while you were mowing the lawn?" she asked the person on the other end of the phone. "No, they're not abandoned. Their mother will come back at night to feed them, so just leave them be."

"Bunnies," Ivy whispered, and Ezra nodded. One of the things they'd learned in their volunteer training was when to help an animal and when to leave it alone. People who found baby bunnies in a nest often worried they had been abandoned. But it was actually fine for the babies to be alone. Mother cottontails often left them in a nest during the day and came back to feed them at night.

"No worries. Have a great day." Miss Alex put down her phone and turned to Ezra, Ivy, and Mom. "Screech owls, right?"

Ezra held out the shoebox. "Two of them."

Miss Alex took the box and headed for the exam room. "Would you like to observe while Doc examines them? She said it was okay."

"Yes, please!" Ezra followed her through the door with Mom and Ivy behind him.

The exam room was full of counters and cages. In the middle was a big metal table where the hospital staff looked over animals when they arrived. From there, animals went to whichever room best fit the care they needed.

The wildlife hospital had a bird room, a reptile room, and a mammal room. There was a nursery for baby animals and a quarantine room where sick animals could be kept alone so they didn't infect others. There was also a kitchen where staff and volunteers prepared the animals' diets each day. Doc spent most of her time in the exam room, especially on busy days like today.

"Let's see how these little ones are doing." She opened the shoebox and lifted out one owl at a time. Miss Alex held the little owls while Doc examined them. They looked up at her with big wide eyes, calling as if they were asking "Where are we? Who are you? Where are our parents?"

Chirrup! Chirrup!

"They seem hungry," Doc said. "Did you see any parents around?"

Ezra shook his head. "We looked, but the dead pine tree with their nest cavity got knocked down last night. Seems like maybe they got freaked out and flew away."

Doc nodded. "That's a good guess. But hopefully they'll be back. We'll need to observe these two for a bit to make sure they're healthy and strong enough. Then we'll see about rehoming them in your yard."

"How can you do that with their nesting tree gone?" Ivy asked.

"We'll have to offer them a new one," Doc said. "The good news is that Eastern screech owls are happy to nest in home-made boxes. Would you be game to put one up in your yard?"

"Definitely!" Ezra said.

Mom nodded. "We can get that done right away."

"Perfect." Doc looked up at Miss Alex. "Could you please grab them a nest box from the garage?"

Ezra, Ivy, and Mom followed Miss Alex past the big outdoor cages for injured birds that were learning to fly again. That was the last stop before they could return to the wild. Ezra spotted an enormous bald eagle on one of the perches. It looked at him with stern yellow eyes as they passed.

Behind the hospital was a big garage and workshop with all kinds of supplies. "Let's see," Miss Alex said. "I thought we had plenty of nest boxes, but I guess we've gone through a lot lately." She crouched to look under a shelf. "Aha! Here we go. The last one."

The owl nesting box was made of plain-looking wood. It was similar to a regular birdhouse but a little bigger. Near the top was a hole about the size of Ezra's fist. Miss Alex handed them a bag of wood chips, too. "You can put some of these in the bottom of the box for bedding."

They loaded up the van and waved to Miss Alex, who said they could stop by tomorrow to see if the owls were ready to go home.

Ezra was quiet on the car ride home. He was glad the owls were at the hospital where they'd get the care they needed. But they were so small. It had to be scary in there with all the bigger birds. He hoped they'd be all right.

CHAPTER 5
Owl the Worst Jokes

As soon as they got home, Ezra, Ivy, and Mom scouted the back yard for a good tree.

"Think the owls would like this one?" Ezra asked, pointing to a tall pine.

Mom nodded. "Their old nesting cavity

was in a pine snag, so that makes sense. And this is close to their old tree, too. That's important."

They met Dad in the garage and set to work gathering supplies. Mom and Dad had built a whole garden shed together, so they had lots of tools. Dad grabbed the ladder. Mom handed Ezra the cordless drill to carry, and Ivy got a box full of brackets and screws. Then they all tromped back into the trees.

Ezra poured some of the wood chips into the bottom of the box. "It doesn't look very comfortable," he said. "Should I put in a towel or something, too?"

Mom shook her head. "Screech owls aren't fussy. They don't actually build nests. They tend to use whatever's already in a cavity, so that should be fine."

"I hope the owls like their new house," Ivy said as Mom climbed the ladder.

"I bet they will," Dad said as Ezra handed up the box. "They'll probably have a party in here. It'll be a real *hoot*."

Ezra groaned. Puns were Dad's favorite thing. They were in for at least a week of bad owl jokes.

"Does this look about right?" Mom asked, holding the box in place. "Miss Alex said it should be at least ten feet off the ground with a clear path for the owls to fly into the opening."

"Looks right to me," Ivy said.

"I didn't bring a measuring tape," said

Dad. "Guess we'll have to *wing it.*" He laughed at his joke. "Get it? Wing it? Because owls have wings?"

Ezra rolled his eyes. "Looks good, Mom."

Ivy handed up a bracket and screw, and Ezra passed Mom the drill so she could secure the box against the tree's shaggy bark. After the last screw was in, she climbed down and looked up at her work. "I'd totally move in there."

"Yeah, but you're not an owl," Ezra said as they headed back to the house. He kept searching the tree branches as he walked. Were the owlets' parents still around somewhere? Or did the storm that toppled their tree scare them off? Would they return once their babies were back in the nest?

Ivy and Dad put the tools away while Ezra helped Mom make some sandwiches for lunch.

Ezra wolfed down his turkey and cheese and two apples. He was so worried about the owls that he'd forgotten about the long skinny birthday gift on the counter until Dad plopped it in his lap. "Here you go, birthday boy!"

Ezra unwrapped it and tried to sound excited.

"Thanks!" He *should* have been excited. It was one of the fancy new composite bats that everyone wanted. They were pretty expensive and often sold out. "I can't believe you found one."

Dad beamed. "It's secondhand. I picked it up at the used sporting goods store, but it's like new. The manager said it had just come in."

Ezra stood up and held the bat in position. It felt good in his hands. And he knew that the new bats had a bigger "sweet spot" that made it easier to connect with a pitch.

But when Ezra imagined going to practice with all of the middle school kids tomorrow, he still felt like an owlet in a room full of eagles. How was he going to keep up?

CHAPTER 6
An Owl Pellet Mystery

Later that afternoon, Ezra's friend Gus invited him to the park. Gus was moving up to the new baseball team, too. But he was actually excited about it.

"Is your homework done?" Dad asked.

That was a good question. Ezra didn't

like to think about homework on week-
ends, so he checked his assignment book.

Science: Our backyards, driveways,
and sidewalks are home to many
animals and plants. Spend ten
minutes outside this weekend and
make a list of all the animals and
plants you identify. Bonus: Collect
something from your outdoor space
for our neighborhood nature
display! (No living things, please!)

"I just have one quick thing for science," Ezra said. "Can I go?"

"Homework first, even on your birthday," Dad said. So Ezra called Gus, who

agreed to come over to observe the yard and see the new owl box. Then they'd walk to the park together.

"Mosquito!" Gus slapped his arm. "Does that count?"

"Yep." Ezra wrote it down. He'd started his list with the screech owls, even though they weren't in the yard right now.

Gus walked over to check out the new nesting box. "So when are your baby owls coming back?"

"Depends," Ezra said as a squirrel ran across the yard. He wrote it down. "Hopefully this week if they're doing well."

"Where's their old tree?" Gus asked.

"Over here." Ezra led Gus to the fallen

pine. A brown anole lizard was perched on it. Ezra jotted that down, too.

He poked around in the grass, hoping for some feathers for extra credit. But all he found was a brown clump with fur sticking out of it.

"Owl poop?" Gus guessed.

"Maybe." Ezra poked it with a stick. He wasn't sure his teacher, Miss Griffin, would give credit for poop, but it was worth a try. He flicked it onto his notebook with the stick and went inside to find a plastic bag.

Mom glanced over from the birthday cake she was icing. "Oh! You found an owl pellet!"

"Is that what they call their poop?" Ezra asked.

"It's not poop," she said. "When owls eat, they cough up the fur and bones—all the parts they can't digest. It comes out in a little pellet."

"Cool!" Ezra was pretty sure Miss Griffin would think so, too. He tucked his list and the owl pellet into his backpack and headed to the park with Gus.

They played catch for a while and then pitched to each other for batting practice. Ezra had to admit his new bat was pretty cool. It was light for its size and didn't sting his hands when he hit the ball. He got a couple good hits in before it was time to go home for dinner and cake.

But Gus wasn't a middle school pitcher. Things would be different at practice tomorrow.

Miss Griffin's fifth-grade classroom was bustling with activity Monday morning. Lots of kids brought in leaves from their yards. Ellen brought in a dead palmetto bug from her sidewalk, and Riley brought a snakeskin that a garter snake had shed.

"I have something, too." Ezra pulled out the bag with the owl pellet and explained what it was. Not only did Miss Griffin give him credit, she got *really* excited. Who knew that owl puke could impress your teacher so much?

"Let's put today's math lesson on hold." Miss Griffin turned to rummage in her supply cupboard. She was always changing plans when something interesting came up. She called those times "genius moments."

"Aha! Here it is." She pulled out a box labeled OWL PELLET MYSTERY, opened it up, and unwrapped a pellet bigger than the one Ezra had brought in.

"Dude, did you *buy* that owl puke?" Gus asked.

Miss Griffin laughed. "The school did. It's a science kit!"

"I am *not* touching owl poop," Tony said.

Ezra corrected him. "Puke. Not poop."

"And this one has been sterilized," Miss Griffin promised. "No germs. Just clues!" She gathered the class around, and everyone took turns pulling the pellet apart and poking it with tweezers. Ezra picked out a tiny skull bone.

"Whoa! Looks like this owl ate . . ." He used the chart that came with the kit to match it. "A mole?"

"Or a mouse?" Ha-Yoon pointed to another skull on the chart. It was a better match.

Ezra wondered if his owls liked mice, too. He'd have to ask Doc about that when they stopped by the wildlife hospital later.

He hoped the owlets were doing all right. Thinking of them in the bird room with all those bigger raptors made him feel a little woozy. Maybe because it reminded him that baseball practice with the middle schoolers was only a few hours away.

CHAPTER 7
Coming Up Short

R eady? Go!"

Ezra ran down the sidewalk as fast as he could, racing toward the light-up speed sign the police had set up to make drivers go slower near the school. Gus had challenged him to see who could get the fastest time on their way to the park for practice.

Ezra pumped his legs harder. His baseball cap blew off, and his legs burned as he passed the sign.

He slowed down, panting, and looked back. He'd been running at full speed, but the sign didn't even light up.

"You weren't fast enough to trigger it," said Gus, whose dad was a city police officer. He was always bragging that he knew how the radar worked.

"My turn!" Gus backed up to get a good running start. Then he took off, racing toward the sign.

Just as he ran past it, a car drove by on the street. The sign lit up.

YOUR SPEED
20MPH

"Woohoo!" Gus pumped his fist.

"That was the car," Ezra said.

"Nah," said Gus. "It was totally me."

Ezra knew that wasn't true, but he envied Gus's confidence. Gus wasn't any older or taller than Ezra, but he didn't seem worried about the new team at all.

Ezra sighed and looked down at his sneakers. They definitely weren't fast enough for the big-kid baseball league, and neither was he.

Luckily, he got a break when they got to the park.

"We're not running a full practice today," said Coach Farley. "You'll have a chance to toss the ball around, but first I want to go over rules and share plans for the season."

Coach went through a list of rules about missing practices, coming prepared to play, and treating everyone with respect. "But we're more than baseball players," he said. "We're members of this community. That's important to me, so I like to do a small team service project the first Tuesday of each month, when you get out of school early for teacher meetings. It's a

way to help out. Tomorrow, we'll be cleaning up the school playground, but I'd like
you to bring ideas for next month."

Then they went around the circle so
players could introduce themselves.
Everyone was in middle school, except
Gus and Ezra and a tall girl named Marcy.
She didn't look worried at all.

Coach Farley hit everyone a few ground
balls, and then they paired up for catch.
Ezra played with Gus. When they realized
Marcy didn't have a partner, they invited
her to join them and made a triangle.

"I'm a pitcher," she said, zinging the
ball into Ezra's glove. "What position do
you guys play?"

"First base," said Gus.

"I don't know. I mean, I was shortstop on my old team, but . . ." Ezra looked around at the middle school players towering over him. He may have been shortstop last year, but this year he was just plain short.

At the end of practice, Coach Farley blew his whistle to call them together. "Before you leave, I want to talk about the most important quality of a good ball player."

Ezra noticed some of the other kids standing up taller, as if they already knew they had that quality. Strength or speed or whatever it was. Ezra felt himself shrink a little.

"That quality is a growth mindset," said Coach. "I don't ever want to hear you put yourselves down out there. We're all works in progress. So instead of saying 'I can't throw a curveball,' try saying 'I can't throw a curveball . . . yet.' Leave room for the possible, all right?"

Ezra liked that idea, even if not much felt possible for him on this team.

At least, not yet.

CHAPTER 8
A Flutter of Hope

Your practice was so long!" Ivy complained when Ezra got into the car. "I've been *waiting* to go see our owls."

"Oh!" Ezra perked up. "Do they get to go home today?"

"That'll be up to Doc," Mom said as she

pulled out of the parking lot. "But if they're healthy and eating well, it should be a go." She stopped for a red light and looked at Ezra in the rearview mirror. "How was practice with the new team?"

"Fine." He'd just spent an hour feeling small. He didn't want to spend *more* time talking about it. "We dissected an owl pellet in school today."

"The one you found?" Mom asked.

"No. Another one Miss Griffin had in some kit. She said it had been sterilized."

Mom nodded. "That makes sense. What had that owl been eating?"

"Mice, we think. Maybe a vole."

"Cool!" Ivy said. "I wish we did stuff like that in my class."

Ezra pulled the bag with the original owl pellet from his backpack. "We could take this one apart at home later. Miss Griffin made a copy of the chart to identify bones."

"Just remember that one hasn't been sterilized, so it'll be germy," Mom said as they pulled up to the wildlife hospital. "It's okay if you wear gloves and do it outside, though."

Ivy clapped her hands. "We can do that right after we re-nest our owls!"

But that plan didn't work out. As soon as they walked into the hospital, Miss Alex shook her head. "I was hoping they'd be

eating up a storm and ready to go by now,"
she said. "But I'm afraid they're not there
yet. Doc thinks they may have been hurt
when the tree fell. They're hopeful little
guys, though. Keep trying to flutter their
wings, but . . ." She shrugged.

"So we have to wait?" Ezra asked. He
tried to be patient, but he was worried.
"How long will the parents hang around
looking for them?"

"No more than two or three days," Miss
Alex said. "So the sooner we get them
back, the better their chances of being
reunited. Let's hope they're doing better
by tomorrow."

"Can we see them?" Ivy looked as if
she were about to cry.

Ezra felt that way, too. "Just for a minute?"

Miss Alex smiled. "Let me check with the boss." She ducked into the exam room, then came back and motioned them to follow her into the nursery.

The room was bustling with activity. Doc had called in extra volunteers.

"It's baby season," Miss Alex explained. "And that storm over the weekend did a job on nests, so we have a lot of little ones to take care of this week. A couple of osprey chicks. Some songbirds. And even more owls." She motioned for Ivy and Ezra to follow her to a cage in the corner.

The two tiny owls were inside, snuggled in a little basket someone had

knitted. Volunteers made all kinds of cozy containers and mini sleeping bags for the baby animals. The owls seemed pretty happy, but they weren't moving much. The little one was holding his head to one side. It made him look confused, as if the whole situation was just overwhelming. Ezra knew what that felt like.

"Is Doc going to give them more medicine?" Ivy asked.

Miss Alex nodded. "She has some ideas for how to help. But we'll have to wait and see. I'll call tomorrow with an update, okay?"

Mom nodded and headed for the door with Ivy. But Ezra stayed back a minute, staring at the littlest owl.

Chirrup!

The owlet gave a hopeful little flutter and then plopped back down in the basket. It looked up with big round eyes as if to say, *What's wrong with me? I'm trying my best and still not measuring up.*

Ezra felt so sad for the owlet. "Get better, okay?" he whispered into the basket. "And then we can take you home."

CHAPTER 9
Secret Plans and Pop Flies

After dinner, Ezra and Ivy went outside to dissect their owl pellet. This one didn't have nearly as many bones. Mom said that might be because the owl was eating softer prey like worms and insects that didn't have bones or fur.

"Can we stay out a while to see if we hear the owl parents?" Ezra asked.

Mom smiled. "Fifteen minutes, okay?"

"Deal."

Ivy claimed the swing seat and cozied up to read her book. Ezra settled into one of the lounge chairs.

Ivy read, and Ezra waited. But all he heard was the rustle of her turning pages. He must have sighed.

"What's wrong?" Ivy asked.

"I'm worried about our owls," Ezra said. "I hate waiting. I wish we could do *something*." He meant to stop talking, but the rest spilled out. "Also, baseball isn't going very well and I feel like I'm not good at anything anymore."

"I feel that way about volleyball sometimes, too. But you're good at lots of things.
Like making stuff. And eating cake." Ivy
put her book down and looked out into the
trees. "I know what you mean about the
owls, though. We don't even know if
the parents survived that storm. It stinks
when there's nothing you can do to help."
She twisted the corner of a pool towel
draped over the fence. And that gave Ezra
an idea.

"Wait . . . remember when you and your
friends collected all those towels for the
wildlife hospital? We could do something
like that!"

"We got a *lot* of towels," Ivy said. "They
probably don't need more yet."

"They need owl boxes, though." And Ezra *was* good at building things. "Remember how they were all out? And Miss Alex said even *more* owlets came in after ours."

Fifteen minutes later, they'd printed out plans for making an owl box. Mom and Dad had all the tools needed and promised to help cutting lumber. "I have tomorrow off, so I can pick up everything we need in the morning," Dad said. "And you only have a half day tomorrow, too. Want to work on this after school?"

"The hospital needs a lot of these, so I was thinking I'd ask my new baseball team if they'd like to help," Ezra said. "Coach said we're doing a service project each month."

"Well, now," said Dad. "It sounds like you and your new coach might be in cahoots on this. Get it? Ca-*hoots*?"

"Dad . . ."

"Sorry," he said, still laughing.

"We were going to clean up the playground tomorrow," Ezra explained, "but the hospital needs these boxes right away. Do you think he might consider switching projects to get these built?"

Dad looked at his watch. "It's super short notice, but I can give him a call to ask. You might not get the whole team, but I bet some kids would come help."

The next day, Coach announced they'd be walking to the wildlife hospital after practice to help build owl boxes. He'd emailed everyone's grown-ups last night to get the okay. "Ezra, your dad says you have directions printed out for us, right?"

Ezra nodded. "They're not too hard to make. My dad picked up the lumber, and he'll have the pieces cut for us —that's the tricky part. We'll just need the team to put the boxes together."

"And real owls are going to live in them?" asked one of the sixth-grade boys.

Ezra nodded.

"Cool!" said a seventh grader.

"Pretty *owlsome* project if you ask me!"

Coach said. He and Dad were going to get along just fine. "Now who's ready to scrimmage?"

Everyone cheered except Ezra. But he grabbed his glove and followed Gus into the outfield. For the first few weeks, everyone would try out different positions. Ezra understood that newer players ended up in the outfield a lot, but he hoped that wouldn't be permanent. He hated pop flies. There was nothing worse than having that ball coming at you, knowing everything depended on you catching it.

Marcy headed for the pitching mound. A seventh grader named Liam stepped into the batting box, looking super confident. But that changed to a look of surprise when her first pitch zinged past him into the catcher's mitt.

Thwack!

Good job, Marcy, Ezra thought. If she kept pitching like that, maybe he wouldn't have to worry about pop flies.

He was just starting to relax when a short, skinny sixth grader named Amir stepped up to bat. The pitch was a little low, but he hit it perfectly.

Crack!

The ball made a beeline for Ezra. His heart jumped into his throat. His feet felt rooted in the grass.

Just catch it, he told himself. *Go! You can do this. Just—*

"Got it!" Gus darted in front of him,

caught the ball, and threw it to second base, keeping Amir to a single.

"Nice catch!" Coach called. "But let's make sure we give everyone a chance to play their position. Next one is yours, Ezra!"

Ezra nodded and gave Coach what he hoped was a confident wave. Inside, he felt the opposite of confident.

Not here, Ezra thought to himself as Marcy pitched to the next batter. Luckily, she struck him out and that ended the inning.

When it was Ezra's turn at bat, he let three perfectly good pitches go by and struck out.

Ezra scuffed his feet all the way back to the dugout. He should have been ready. He'd worked hard at practice. He had all the right gear. But apparently, those fancy new bats only worked if you also had the confidence to swing them.

CHAPTER 10
Projects and Possibilities

There was double good news at the wildlife hospital that afternoon. Doc was thrilled to have so many workers building nesting boxes in the garage.

"They'll be put to good use," she said. "We admitted three more owlets today.

Someone cut down a tree in his yard and never even saw them until they were on the ground."

"How are *our* owls doing?" Ezra asked.

That was the other good news. They were both healthy enough to be re-nested!

"We'll send them home with you tonight," Doc said. "But first we're going to make sure they have a good meal. In fact, it's time for us to feed them now. If you're quiet, you can come in and watch."

They all put down their tools and followed Doc to the bird room. Miss Alex was holding both owls in their snuggly little basket.

Doc picked up a small dish of cut-up

pieces of mouse and picked one up with a pair of tweezers. "We feed them little bites, just like their mother would." She held the mouse tidbit out to the bigger owlet, who devoured it.

The little owl's head was still tilted a bit. But when Doc offered him a bite of mouse, he gobbled it right up, too.

"Good job," Ezra whispered.

"Little dudes are hungry," Gus said.

Doc nodded. "That's a great sign." She looked up from the owlets. "Your nesting box is already up and ready to go, right?"

Ezra nodded.

"And have you heard or seen any sign of the parents?" she asked.

"Nope," Ivy said.

"Not yet," Ezra said, to leave room for the possible.

"That's okay," Doc said. "Sometimes they stay hidden. When those babies get back to the yard and start calling for them . . . that's when they'll show themselves, if they're still around."

"They *have* to come back," Ivy said.

Miss Alex put a hand on her shoulder. "I sure hope they do. But these little ones have been out of the nest longer than we'd like. We'll have to wait and see."

What if the parents were already gone? Ezra watched the owlets finish their supper and swallowed a lump in his throat. He didn't want to cry in front of his team.

Besides, he wasn't a little kid. He was a fifth grader. He knew that wildlife rescue stories didn't always have happy endings. But he so hoped this one would. Those little owls were working so hard to go home. It would be so unfair if they made it back and their parents didn't return.

The rest of the afternoon was a buzz of activity—literally. Dad's circular saw hummed as he finished cutting the wood. Mom joined them after her teacher meetings and fired up her new bandsaw to cut a round hole in each box's front piece so the owls could fly in and out.

Ezra loved being with his baseball team at the wildlife hospital. He felt way more confident here than at the baseball diamond, and using tools was easier than swinging fancy new baseball bats. Not everybody felt that way, though.

"Dude, I have made a mess of this," said Amir, the sixth grader who hit the ball that Ezra didn't catch.

"You've got that roof piece upside down," Ezra said. "Here . . ." He helped Amir get his nest box pieces in order so he could try again.

"Can you look at mine, too?" asked Gus, whose opening was in the wrong place.

"It needs to be like this," Ezra said, turning it. "That way, the baby owls can't fall out once they're in the nest. They'll

only be able to get up there after they've learned to fly a little."

"So you and your sister volunteer here?" asked Marcy, as an egret called from one of the big outdoor flight cages.

Ezra nodded. "Mostly we just help Mom and Dad. But when we're in high school we'll get to do more with the actual animals. I really want to do that. I'm not sure if I'll keep playing baseball or not."

"Really?" said one of the seventh graders. Ezra thought his name was Jesse. "I've seen you practicing in the park. You've got a great swing!"

Ezra shook his head. "I struck out the one time I was at bat."

"Let me guess," Jesse said. "New bat?"

Ezra smiled. "For my birthday last weekend. I haven't figured it out . . . yet."

"I have the same one—a hand-me-down from my cousin. It's awesome but it took me a while to get used to it. I can give you some pointers if you want."

"Yeah?" Ezra liked the idea of that. "Thanks!"

"But you gotta help me with this first." Jesse held up his lopsided owl box. "I'm apparently not great at carpentry . . . yet."

CHAPTER 11
Homecoming

After the boxes were finished, Doc came out to thank them. "Thanks so much for your work today!"

The team took pictures with Doc and the owl boxes. Then everyone went to Ezra and Ivy's house for pizza. Including

Miss Alex. It was time for the owlets to go home.

Miss Alex brought them out to the yard in the little knit basket. When Ezra peeked inside, the littlest owl was flapping his wings. "He looks stronger already!" Ezra said.

"Little dude's ready to go," Gus said.

Miss Alex nodded. "It's time to get them both back out in the world."

Mom set up the ladder so Miss Alex could ease the owlets into their nesting box. She took a picture of them for Ezra and Ivy. They looked mostly happy in there, Ezra decided. Maybe a little unsettled, but at least they had each other. And hopefully, soon, their parents would return.

"Should we set up a camera or something so we'll know if they come back?" What Ezra really wanted to do was watch the nest all night, but he knew he couldn't do that.

"Nope. We have a low-tech solution that works quite well." Miss Alex pointed to a branch on the ground. "Could you please break off a twig for me?"

Ezra snapped off a skinny twig and handed it up to Miss Alex. She broke it in half and arranged the pieces and wedged them into the opening of the nest box to make an X. "The little owls haven't fledged yet, so they can't fly up here. So if these twigs are gone in the morning, we'll know their parents have come back to feed them."

"What if they're not?" Ivy asked.

"Then I'll stop by to feed the owlets tomorrow and we'll try again." Miss Alex climbed down the ladder. "But if the parents don't return, we'll have to bring them back to the wildlife hospital to raise them there until they can hunt on their own."

"It would be better if their parents could teach them to hunt," Ezra said.

Miss Alex nodded. "Let's hope for the best. Thank you again for all of your help!" She took a slice of pizza to go and headed home.

Ezra waved as she pulled out of the driveway. But he couldn't stop looking back at the X in the nesting box, sending silent messages to the owl parents, wherever they were.

Your babies are home.

Please come back.

Ezra and his team went inside and dug into their pizza. They talked about their favorite pro baseball players while Dad and Coach made more terrible owl puns.

"This guy is a hoot!" Dad said, slapping Coach on the back.

It was starting to get dark when the grown-ups came to pick everybody up. Ezra walked outside with them. When the last car drove off, he wandered into the backyard. There was enough light to see that the twigs were still in place. Every once in a while, the babies would call from inside.

Chirrrrrup!

Chirrrrrup!

Ezra sighed and went inside. He was cleaning up plates and pizza boxes when a different sound floated in the open window. A trill that wasn't quite so high pitched.

He turned to Ivy. "Did you hear that?"

Her eyes lit up and she nodded. "Mom, was that one of the adult owls? Can we check?"

"It might have been," Mom said. "But let's leave the owls alone tonight. If the parents are back, they'll want to feed their babies without anyone shining lights around. You can check the twigs in the morning."

It took Ezra a long time to fall asleep. When he finally did, he dreamed about baseball. In the dream, he was on his old team, hitting a home run. But when he rounded third base and headed for home, some of his new teammates were waiting to high-five him.

He woke up actually looking forward to that afternoon's practice. Then he remembered the owls, ran downstairs, and burst out the back door in his pajamas.

Ivy was already outside with a pair of binoculars aimed at the tree. There were no *chirrups*. No hungry little chirps. Just early-morning quiet.

"Well?" Ezra asked. She handed them to him, and he looked.

The twigs were gone.

CHAPTER 12
The Sky's the Limit

Chirirrrrrrup!

The little owl stared up at the circle of sky. The circle looked different in this new nest cavity—more even and round—but the sky was the same.

So was the brother who kept shoving him. They were both hungry.

Chirirrrrrrup!

When they'd first landed on the rough wood chips in this new cavity, they were confused. Their bellies were full of mouse pieces they got from the silver pointy beak, and that was good. It took their mother a while to find them.

The owlets had huddled together all that first night. They'd watched the sky circle turn from bright blue to dark blue to black with pinpricks of light, and still, she hadn't come.

They'd called and called, and just as the light began to return, in she flew. She fussed over them for a moment and then let out a call of her own, a trilling *whinny* into the twilight that brought their father with a fresh-caught mouse.

Now the little owl could hold his own, claiming space for himself as he and his brother pushed and shoved for bites. What's more, he was almost ready to fly.

He'd been practicing the whole time he was away, fluffing his feathers, flapping his wings until he lifted off the ground, just a bit. Each time a little higher.

The little owl watched his father flutter up to the perch and fly off again. Perhaps later he would bring back a lizard or a worm.

The owlet flapped his wings the way his father had. He fluttered them faster, then faster still, and found himself rising in the nest.

Up . . . up . . . up! Until he was perched on the edge of the opening and the sky was everywhere. Not just a circle. A wide-open world. Before long, he'd be able to explore it all.

One day soon, he'd fly through the trees like his parents. One day soon, he would hunt on his own. He would perch on a branch, watching and listening and waiting. One day soon, he would swoop silently down and rise with a mouse or lizard in his strong talons.

The little owlet looked out through the shadows and trees. Then he fluttered his

wings and dropped to the wood chips to give his big brother a shove.

Chirirrrrrrup!

It was awfully good to be home.

AUTHOR'S NOTE

This story was inspired by the wildlife and staff at von Arx Wildlife Hospital at the Conservancy of Southwest Florida, where I serve as a volunteer. One of my jobs at the beginning of each shift is preparing diets for the animals in the hospital that day. Every time I feed a mouse to an Eastern screech owl, I'm reminded of the little

owlets I met when I was doing research at the wildlife hospital in April 2022.

The owl babies in this story were inspired by real owl siblings that were nesting in the hollow of a pine snag and ended up on the ground when it fell. Once the hospital staff ensured they were healthy, the owlets were re-nested in a box just like the ones Ezra makes in the story. I tagged along on that mission, tromping into the woods behind a rural home in

Collier County, Florida, as wildlife hospital volunteer Tim Thompson headed out with his tool belt to set up the owlets' new home.

Ezra's experience of finding the owls while he was playing outside is also inspired by a Conservancy wildlife success story. That same year, a boy named Cooper was practicing golf in his yard when he went to pick up a golf ball in the lawn—and realized it was a baby owl!

The owlet had fallen from an unstable nest in an old woodpecker hole in a Canary palm, so it couldn't be returned to its old nest without running the risk that the same thing would happen again. So wildlife hospital volunteers put up a nesting box for the owl family instead.

Three weeks later, the owlet fledged. Later that spring, I visited the family's yard and spotted the owlet perched in a tree not far from the nesting box, with his parents looking on from other trees nearby.

These Eastern screech owls were just a few of the more than four thousand animals admitted to the von Arx Wildlife Hospital each year. I'm grateful to the hospital staff for their amazing work with wildlife and for their generosity in sharing their knowledge and stories. Thanks especially to hospital director Joanna Fitzgerald and longtime volunteer Tim Thompson. You can read more about the wildlife hospital's work here:

https://conservancy.org/our-work /wildlife-rehabilitation/.

Here are some resources to check out if you'd like to learn more about owls, dissect an owl pellet, or build a nesting box of your own:

"Eastern Screech Owl." All About Birds.

The Cornell Lab. https://www
.allaboutbirds.org/guide/Eastern
_Screech-Owl/lifehistory

Eastern Screech-Owl Nest Box Plan and
Information from NestWatch. The
Cornell Lab of Ornithology. https://
nestwatch.org/learn/all-about
-birdhouses/birds/eastern-screech-owl/

*Owling: Enter the World of the Mysterious
Birds of the Night* by Mark Wilson
(Storey Publishing, 2019).

Owl Pellet Kit from Cornell Lab. https://
www.birds.cornell.edu/k12/owl-pellet
-kit/

BE A WILDLIFE HERO

If you love the idea of helping owls and other birds, you can be a wildlife hero, too. You may not be able to work directly with animals at your local wildlife hospital— many will want you to wait until you're a teenager—but there are lots of other ways to help.

1. Collect donations! Nearly all

wildlife hospitals rely on
donations from the public. They
can always use money to pay for
food and supplies, so donations
are appreciated. You might
choose to hold a bake sale or set
up a lemonade stand to raise
money for your local wildlife
hospital. Or, if you'd like to donate
to the von Arx Wildlife Hospital at
the Conservancy of Southwest
Florida, you can do that here:
https://6890a.blackbaudhosting
.com/6890a/RES-WILDLIFE.

2. If you live in an area that's safe for
owls, consider putting up a

nesting box. You might just attract a breeding pair to your backyard. You can find directions for building different kinds of nesting boxes online and in the link on page 106. It's also a good idea to attach a guard to keep predators away from the box so they don't eat the eggs and baby owls.

3. You can also make your yard owl-friendly by leaving dead trees standing if you can. This might not always be possible, such as when trees are in danger of falling. But trees that aren't in danger of falling on homes or

people can be left alone to
become homes for wildlife.

4. Turn off the lights! Owls' eyes are
   adapted to help them hunt in
   almost complete darkness. Light
   pollution from outdoor lights on
   porches and garages can
   confuse owls as they're trying to
   hunt. Don't leave lights on all
   night unless absolutely
   necessary.

5. Keep pets indoors at night.
   Animals like Ezra's neighbor's cat,
   Tabitha, are still predators, and

the cats and dogs we love can be deadly for wildlife.

6. Avoid using poison to control pests. You're probably not in charge of your home's rodent-control plan, but you can ask your grown-ups what they use when mice or rats are spotted around the house. Some kinds of poison don't kill rats and mice right away. Instead, the rodent eats the poison bait and keeps scurrying around outdoors, where it is likely to become prey for a hungry owl, who is then also poisoned. This is

called secondary poisoning, and many hawks and owls die from it each year.

7. Watch birds and participate in citizen science projects. Many groups rely on volunteers to gather data about owl and other bird populations. Check out groups and events like eBird and the Christmas Bird Count to get started. Your observations and data will be used by scientists studying these amazing animals.

Turn the page for a sneak peek at the
next Wildlife Rescue adventure!

CHAPTER 1
Digging a Home

The gopher tortoise flung a claw full of sand out of her burrow. Soon, it would be time to lay her eggs. She would need a soft, wide apron of sand outside the burrow entrance for her nest.

Dig and fling!

Dig and fling!

Sand sprayed out behind her. She was good at this. Her wide front legs and sturdy claws worked like shovels. They were made for digging!

The tortoise had built lots of burrows in her fifteen years. Her first had been a shallow one, just a few meters from the nest where she was born.

Back then, her shell was soft; she had to hide from so many predators! Bobcats and coyotes prowled at night, but she stayed safe inside, out of reach.

She survived.

Now fully grown, she dug longer, deeper burrows. They provided shelter from the sun on the hottest days and protection from the cold on chilly nights. And not just for her! Sometimes she shared her home with burrowing owls or snakes. Beetles and lizards always crawled in, too.

The tortoise had chosen a perfect location for this new burrow: an open sandy lot where the trees had been cleared. Wildflowers and grass sprouted in the sunlight.

Dig and fling!

Dig and fling!

When the tortoise finished, she headed out to graze. Every few steps, she stopped to chomp on mouthfuls of grass. But the tiny purple flowers were her favorite. Fresh and sweet and full of water. Where were they? Every few steps, she stopped to chomp on mouthfuls of grass. But the tiny purple flowers were her favorite. Fresh and sweet and full of water. Where were they?

She lumbered along until she ran out of sand and grass. Cars and trucks zoomed back and forth on the busy road. Just on the other side was an open space with more plants. And was that a patch of purple?

The tortoise stepped onto the hard pavement and hesitated. Too many fast cars filled the street. Some sped past her so closely she felt their hot wind on her face.

Finally, a light over the road changed from green to red, and the cars stopped moving. She waited to see if they would start again, but they just sat there, grumbling and still. The flowers on the other side looked delicious.

The tortoise took another step into the road. Then another. Her claws tapped the asphalt as she plodded along between cars.

She was halfway across when the light turned green.

New York Times bestselling author **KATE MESSNER** is passionately curious and writes books for kids who wonder, too. Her titles include award-winning picture books like *Over and Under the Snow*, *The Next Scientist*, and *The Scariest Kitten in the World* as well as novels for older readers like *All the Answers*, *Breakout*, *Chirp*, and *The Trouble with Heroes*. Kate also writes the popular History Smashers graphic nonfiction series and leads the multi-author team behind The Kids in Mrs. Z's Class chapter books. She lives on Lake Champlain and is a proud Adirondack 46er.

www.katemessner.com
@KateMessner